Rozelle Park.

Part One.

Chapter One.

Awaking of the Old Oak Tree.

As the sun dips below the horizon, a serene shine envelops all over Rozelle Park casting a warm glow. In a silent witness to the unfolding magic, an old oak tree stands steadfast. The carvings adorn with their weathered bark seems to come alive, and the animals calls their tree home begun to talk. Who is awake from their slumber, ready for another round of their secret conversations. Perched high up in the tree, a carving of a wise barn owl called Barney wake up from his peaceful slumber. Barney blinks his green eyes as he surveys the park below. On his left side, a naughty squirrel named Peaches, scurries' up and down the trunk, with her tiny paws in a constant motion as she searches for nuts to store for the impending winter. To the left of Peaches, there is a Hand-carved in the wood, he displays a pocket watch, which nestles in his palm. The engraving on his wrist with the initials "P B," hinting at a forgotten pass and the stories waiting to be discovered. Just below Barney, two faces etched into the trunk gazed out with a puzzling expression, labelled "Lefty Face" and "Righty Face." The carve figures, including a delicate Thistle and a sturdy Acorn, seem to possess a secret connection. As the evening settles and the park gates closes for the night, an enchantment, swept over the carvings, stirs to life; with their wooden frame animated with hidden energy. Barney, the ever-wise guardian with his cheerful chirping of, "T' wit, T' woos, T' wit, T' woos." With a hint of irritation for being disturbed.

Barney replies. "Good evening, Peaches."

Peaches greets him, with her voice full of excitement. "Hi!"

The stage is set for an extraordinary night in Rozelle Park, where the carve figures converse in secret whispers in the breeze, and the magical essence of the park Intertwines with the lives of its inhabitants. Little did they know, the coming night brings forth a new mystery, a tale that binds them together in unexpected ways. And so, the story of Rozelle Park begins, its secrets waiting to be unravelled by those willing to listen, watching and delve into the realms in which the reality and enchantment coexist.

Barney, still a bit grumpy from being woken up, scolds Peaches with a stern tone, "What are you doing? You just woke me up." He stands there, visibly confused by the unfolding disturbance.

Peaches, realising her mistake, quickly exchanges greetings, "Hello, hi!" and apologises with a remorseful tone, "Sorry, I must dash, to search for my nuts to add to my cache."

Barney, with his irritation softens, responds, "Well, that is understandable. Thank you very much for waking me up, Peaches."

Peaches, eager to make amends, nods, and replies, "I'm off now, see you later."

With that, Peaches scurries away, her tail disappearing into the shadows of Rozelle Park. Barney watches her go, his own eyes fill with mixture of annoyance and the affections of his life. He knows Peaches meant no harm, and her energetic nature brings a sense of life and vigour to the old oak tree.

Barney settles on his perch and ponders with the events of the evening. He wonders what adventures and the mysteries waits for him in the moonlight hours of Rozelle Park.

With a gentle sway of his carved head, he prepares himself for the night ahead, ready to embrace the magic and the secrets that will unfold beneath the eerie canopy.

The night deepens, shrouded Rozelle Park into darkness, Barney resumes his vigilant has he watches over Rozelle Park. Peaches is busily collecting her nuts; her destinies tangles with the change and embrace of the Old Oak tree and surrounding of mysteries, and Barney's sensation slightly irritated due to the earlier interruption and turns his attention towards Hand and asks, "What's the time?"

Hand slowly rotating his wrist, causing the aged wood, to emit a creaking sound and shows the pocket watch reveals the time as 9 30 P M. Barney lets out with a dismayed cry, "I usually wake up around eleven! Thank you, Peaches!" Then he continues with his T wit, T woos, trying to resume of his peaceful routine.

However, the commotion catches the attention of Lefty face, who awakens from his slumber with a state of annoyance. He grumbles with the irritation in his voice, "Oh, shut up, Barney! You have just woken me up with all this bickering."

Barney, his carved features ruffled, raises his voice, "Now you know what it's like when the fluffy rodent keeps running up and down the trunk."

Righty face stirs from his slumber, yawns, and interrupts, "Shut up, You two! You also woken me up with all this bickering." He continues, "I'm sick, I'm sick and I'm tired of this!"

Barney protests, "Maybe, I am seemed to bicker? It is Peaches, she always wakes me up! It is only 9 30."

Lefty face shouts back, "Okay, fine! Every day, you always wake me up with your T' wit, T' woos, and you blame it on Peaches. But that is you! You are the one, who keeps on going on and on, and wakes us faces up."

The argument starts to escalate, their voices getting louder, and their frustrations are mounting. The peaceful harmony of the night is shattered by the incessant Bickering. The park remains oblivious to their squabbles, as if it seen all this before. And so, the carvings continue to bicker, getting on each other's nerves, unaware of the passage of time and with the secrets waiting to be discovered in the depths of Rozelle Park.

Chapter Two.

Red-Breasted Robin Flies Overhead:

Unveiling the Tree's Turmoil.

A red-breasted Robin flies past the old oak tree. He cannot help but notices the commotion below. Curiously crossed, he nose-dives down towards the tree, his wings beating rapidly to slow his descent as he approaches. He hears bickering and the arguments from the carvings coming from the trunk below. Without hesitation, the Robin lands gracefully on the outstretched of Hands finger. He still shows his pocket watch towards Barney. The Robin cocks its head to one side, taking in the scene before him. Lefty Face and Righty Face are still bickering together, their carved faces consorts with angers of frustration. Meanwhile, Barney Continues to make his usual T' wit, T' woos sounds, unfazed by the commotion around him. The Robin chirps softly to get his attention, "Chirpy, Chirpy, Cheep, Cheep."

As Barney turns his head and looks up, to his surprised to see a small bird perched on top of Hand's finger. He greets Robin with a deep rumble in his voice, "Hello there. What brings you here?"

Robin, "Chirps" in response to Barney's statement.

Barney chuckle is and says, "Ah, I see. You are curious?" He continues, "Well, there is always something interesting happening around here. You're welcome to stay if you'd like to find out more."

Curiously, Robin asks, "What's going on?"

Lefty Face lets out a sigh and replies,' "It is a long story."

Barney interrupts, declaring, "No, it is not! It all started with Peaches waking me up," and he continues, "Then, I wake the faces up with my T wit, T woos calls, infuriating them all with my persistence."

Righty Face chimes in, "And that's when we all start bickering."

The Robin nods his head and responds, "Well, that is not genuinely nice. You should all try to have a good relationship with each other."

Lefty Face look at Robin and acknowledges, "You're right. We should all try to get along."

Just as the conversation unfolds, Peaches returns to the old oak tree with the nuts she had collected for her impending winter.

Robin notices and greets her, "Hi. You must be Peaches? My name is Robin."

Peaches replies with a simple, "Hi!"

Robin has been curious about Peaches, and he asks, "I have a question for you. Do you always get up early?"

Peaches responds, "Yes, I do wake up early when the park reopens to the public, and I stay up in this tree all day long." She explains further, "However, this is not the ideal time to forage and store nuts in my cache for winter. The ideal time is when the park closes, and the public departs." Peaches concludes, "That's when I can go freely foraging to stock up my cache for the upcoming winter."

Robin nods in an understanding and remarks, "Oh, I see."

Peaches express her frustration, stating, "But lately, the carvings always seem to wake up well after the park closes. Disturbing me, before I can go off to sleep."

Robin contemplates the issue, and says, "We have a situation here."

Peaches express her frustration, stating, "They are constantly bickering and making noises. It is not fair to me, as the carvings do not require food or water." She then adds, "The old oak tree provides the nutrients they need, but It's nearly impossible not to disturb them."

Robin listens to Peaches' words, with a sense of empathy fills his tiny heart. The challenge of balancing the needs of the carvings with Peaches' routine becomes apparent. Robin is thinking of contemplating how they could find a solution that will bring the harmony to share their home in the old oak tree. And so, in the depths of Rozelle Park, the carvings, Peaches, and Robin faces a need for understanding with a compromise. As the night progresses, they strive to find a way to coexist peacefully, respecting each other's needs and embracing the unique magic that surrounds them in the enchanting realm of Rozelle Park.

Robin perches on the Hand's finger, he suggests, "Hand, what time does the park shuts and reopens?"

Robin takes flight from Hand's finger and hovers in front of Him, examining the watch. The timepiece indicates that the park shuts at 8 30 PM and reopens at 8 30 A M, exactly twelve hours apart.

This realisation dawns on them, knowing that Peaches has amble time in the morning for her foraging activities.

Turning towards Peaches, Robin asks, "Do the carvings keep you awake all night?"

Peaches shakes her head and says, "No."

Righty Face looks puzzled and asks, "But why would we do that?"

Robin explains, "Because if all of you get up at the same time, then Peaches can forage, and she won't disturb your slumber."

Barney chimes in, "Yeah! We can all benefit from a little peace and quiet."

Gratefully for the suggestion, Peaches thanks Robin for producing the idea. They have decided to try synchronising their sleeping habits with Peaches to achieve a peaceful coexistence. Hand listening to the discussion decide to set the watch alarm for 8 30 PM, ensuring a reminder for the carvings to wake up at the same time before Peaches goes out to forage. With a careful twist of the dial, the soft ticking of the alarm is set. As the decision is made, Robin having fulfilled its purpose of bringing harmony to the group, prepares to leave. Flapping his wings, he takes flight from Hand's finger, bidding a gentle farewell with his chirps. Robin soars into the night sky, disappearing into the darkness. Lefty Face, Righty Face, Barney, and Peaches exchange favourable glances, and they are grateful for Robin's involvement and the newfound plan for peaceful coexistence. The old oak tree stands tall and still, its remaining branches gently swaying in the night breeze as the carvings settle for a shared understanding. And so, with Hand's watch alarm set and with the guidance of Robin's wisdom. Peaches and the Carvings embarks on a new chapter of intertwine existence. The tranquillity of the night will soon be preserved, allowing each inhabitant of Rozelle Park to find their rhythm within the purpose of the magical embrace.

Chapter Three.

Robin Returns:

The Triumph of His Ingenious Scheme.

The carvings wake up to the vibrations of the alarm and gazing upon Peaches, such as she carefully collects for her nuts. Their eyes turn towards the horizon with a breath-taking sunset, paints the sky with vibrant colours and overwhelms with the beauty before them. They cannot help, but yell in unison, their voices blending with their shared astonishment. "Wow!" They scream with their voices harmonising and carrying on the breeze rippling right through Rozelle Park.

Barney with his voice fulfils with amazement, calls out, "Look at those colours! It is like a painting in the sky!"

Peaches pauses from her foraging, with a smile, and nods in agreement, "It's truly remarkable." She says, with her voice filled with wonder. "Nature always captures us."

Lefty Face. With his irritation transforms into appreciation, he adds, "I never thought I'd appreciate something as simple as a sunset, but here we are, witnessing the splendour with all of us together."

Righty Face joins in the chorus, yelling, "Indeed! We have the privilege of experiencing the beauty of nature while fostering a peaceful coexistence." And he adds, "What a blessing, it's has become!"

As the sun dips lower on the horizon, cashing a warm glow over Rozelle Park. Peaches and the carvings stand up with a respect, united in appreciation with the world around them. At that moment, they realise that their journey towards harmony and understanding was about more than just the individual's needs.

It was about embracing the magnificence of life itself and so, with the echoes of joyfulness fulfilling the air. Peaches and the carvings continue to coexist in Roselle Park, their hearts fill with gratitude with the shared moment and the beauty that surrounding them. Together, they also embark with a new evening, ready to embrace the wonders that awaits them, and the nature with the bonding, they have forge in their enchanted home. Robin still harbours with a trace of anger from earlier time, lands on hand's outstretched finger, expecting to find the carvings engage with their usual bickering. However, to his pleasant surprise, he was greeted by a serene atmosphere and the captivating sight of the carvings, immerse with the beauty of the sunset.

Bewildered, yet delighted, Robin wonders, "What is going on here? I thought I was preparing for another round of bickering, but the things have taken a turn for the better."

Barney noticing Robin with a perplex expression, and he let out a chuckle and responds, "Ah! You have missed a quite a development earlier, my feathered friend, we have reconsidered, and we decided to embrace with a more harmonious existence."

Peaches, she is wearing a contented smile, chimes in, "Indeed, Robin. Me and the carvings have come to realise the importance of getting along and respecting one another's needs, we also witness the breath-taking sunset together, and it served as a reminder of the beauty of unity."

Robin's angers dissolves with a sense of relief and curiosity. "That is wonderful to hear! I am glad to see that you all have found a common ground." He also adds, "Can you tell me, how did this transformation come about?"

Lefty Face chimes in, "It is a combination of your wise suggestion and the enchanted sunset itself; we've realised that our bickering and discords were hindering our ability of the appreciation and the world around us."

Righty Face nods in agreement and continues, "You suggest that we synchronise our sleeping schedules with Peaches, so, she doesn't have to rush and disturb of our slumber, it has brought us with a newfound sense of peace and understanding."

Robin, impressed with the carvings' growth and the willingness to change and expresses of gratitude. "I'm glad I played with this part of this transformation; it is heart-warming to witness the power of unity and cooperation."

As the conversation draws to a close, Robin spreads his wings and prepares to fly home, "My friends, it's time for me to bid you, farewell." He continues with, "My hatchlings are waiting for me, but I must say goodbye, you made Rozelle Park, a truly a special place." He also adds, "Keep fostering with the harmony of this peace and I'll be back to check on you very soon."

Robin takes flight, soaring into the fading light of the evening sky. As he journeys on towards his nest, but he cannot help but feel with a real sense of hope and the ultimate optimism for the future of Rozelle Park.

The transformation he witnesses among the carvings and the animals fills with joy. The newfound coexistence and appreciation are a testament to the power of understanding and unity. It is a promising sign that harmony can prevail with the enchanted realm of Rozelle Park.

Peaches and the carvings watches Robin with his graceful departure; their hearts filled with a gratitude for his role in bringing about positive change. They have exchange looks with the determination and knowing that their journey towards harmony was just the beginning.

The bonds they had formed will continue to strengthen, and their shared commitment to a peaceful coexistence will be a guiding light in the days to come.

Meanwhile, as Robin flies' home, and he notice something has catches his eye with the curiosity on the ground. He makes a mental note, and he will explore it further tomorrow, eager to uncover more mysteries in the enchanting world of Rozelle Park.

Chapter Four.

Robins Family:

Hungers for Pursuit.

Next day arrives, the Robin's already hard at work, scouring the ground for seeds, insects, and worms, with the occasional of luck, to find some mealworms. Rozelle Park is alive with activity as visitors of all kind's flocks in and enjoying the park's offerings. Robins tirelessly gather food, ensuring their hatchlings receive the essential nutrients for robust growth and independence. Meanwhile, with a feeding frenzy, ensures as the public partakes with the gift of mealworms placed on the park tables, provided by the diligent park keepers. Daylight hours are bustling with movement and life, reaching its peak from first light until mid-afternoon. This is the busiest time of day, as it becomes with a hub of activity. Robin and his partner, Robina, takes turns to feed their hungry hatchlings, which guarantee of survival with the thriving of the future generations in the park.

It takes about 23 to 25 days for the hatchlings to reach maturity, but after just 13 days, they will leave the nest, embarking on their own adventures while the parents continue to provide nourishment and guidance.

Currently, the Robins are on their second brood of the season, and they are extremely proud, that they already have successfully nurtured four hatchlings.

Their little ones are curious and eager to explore their surroundings, their fluffy feathers signalling their youthful innocence. The day starts to wind down and the time on the watch approaches 8:30 PM, the statues and the carvings in the park seem to come alive with a touch of magic.

Robins escorted by their curious hatchlings, as they venture out from their nest. The little ones hop and flutter about along the ground, also their parents keeping a watchful eye, guiding them through this new world. The park embraces the warmth of the evening as the sun slowly descends, casting a golden glow over the scene. The air is filled with sounds of chirping birds, rustling leaves, and a gentle hum of life in Rozelle Park.

As they soar through the sky, Robin proposes with an adventurous idea, "Robina, what do you say we go on a little adventure? I spotted a peculiar statue last night, and I cannot help it, but wonder what it is all about." He adds, "Let's go check it out!" Robin's voice is filled with excitement, eager to embark on a new exploration.

Robina lets out a sigh, her tone with a hint of frustration as she replies, her feathers slightly fluffed, "Not again. We have these hatchlings to take care of. It is not always convenient for us to go swanning off on your escapades." Her words convey a sense of responsibility and concern for their young.

Robin looks back at the hatchlings, who follow closely behind. With a determine expression on his face, he addresses Robina, "I understand your concerns, but I truly believe they can come with us, it will be a wonderful learning experience for them, besides, they've been cooped up in the nest for quite a while now." He continues, "It's time for them to spread their wings and embark on their own adventure." His voice exudes with an enthusiasm and a sense of excitement for what lies ahead.

Robina hesitates, contemplating Robin's proposal, knowing that his sense of adventure is hard to resist. However, she does not want the hatchlings to come with him and she wants to take them home. Reluctantly, she relents and says, "Okay, I must take the hatchlings home before it gets too late, but I will allow you to go on your own instead."

Robin sets off towards the intriguing statue. His wings carry him through the gentle breeze, while Robina, with her hatchlings, moves along, feeling slightly upset and she also moans, turning back towards the nest, keeping a watchful eye on her departing partner.

Robin approaches the statue; he marvels at its intricate details and unique form. It stands tall and stoic, frozen in time. Robin's curiosity grows, and he cannot resist investigating further. Perching on the statue's, left shoulder, Robin begins to study its features, examine the fine artisanship and contemplating the stories it might hold.

Meanwhile, he huddles close, his eyes wide with wonder as he takes in the mysterious sight, feeling sense of wonder and interest.

Unbeknownst to Robin, back at the nest, Robina cannot shake off her concerns. She frets over the safety and responsibilities' she has towards her precious young. Yet she knows deep down that not allowing them to explore and learning is essential for their growth.

With a heavy heart, Robina settles her hatchlings into the nest, comforting herself with her babies with the knowledge that Robin is a skilled and caring parent. Despite her moaning and feeling of upset, she cannot help but feels a sense of pride in her growing hatchlings. And so, Robin continues to investigate the enigmatic adventure, his curiosity driving him forward.

Robina, torn between worry and trust, patiently waits for his return, understanding that sometimes the best lessons are learnt through exploration and a touch of parental guidance.

Chapter Five.

Robin Quest Unveils:

Major Tom Comes Alive.

During World War One. A British army officer's uniform with a rank of Major wore a double-breasted woollen tunic with brass buttons. The tunic displaying gold oak leaf rank Insignia on the cuffs, indicating the officers rank. Additionally, the tunic features of shoulders straps with a crown and a pip on each, signifying the officer's rank. To complete the uniform, the officers wore a matching woollen trousers with a Sam Browne leather belt, which crosses over the right shoulder. The peaked cap featured a gold embroidered badge representing the officer's regiment. Leather gloves, ankle boots and a swagger stick were also part of the attire. Medals and ribbons were proudly worn on the left chest. While there were slight variations among the regiments and corps, these details remained consistent throughout the British army.

Hand's pocket watch alarm begins to make a sound, it is now 8 30 P M. Major Tom abruptly awakes from his slumber.

He quickly reaches for his orders and begins to read them with a sense of duty. Lost in his thoughts, he suddenly becomes aware of a talking Robin perched nearby.

Robin, noticing Major Tom's astonishment, chirps' curiously, "What are you doing? Are those orders you are reading?"

Astonished, Major Tom's mutters to himself, "Am I truly conversing with a bird? I must be going mad, and this cannot be real!"

Still bewildered by the situation, Major Tom responds, "These orders relate to the activities taking place across the battlefield known as no man's land, the area lies between our trenches and the Germans." He says, "From here, I can even catch a glimpse of the Germans soldiers on the other side."

Robin, with a hint of amusement in his voice, "No man's land? But there is no such thing here in the park." He continues, "All I see is a serene Wee Loch with ducks and swans peacefully swimming and who are these Germans you are speaking of? My name is Robin."

Major Tom confusion deepens as he scans his peaceful surroundings. He realises that his perception has shifted, and the grim reality of war seems to have dissolved into a tranquil scene. With a mixture of relief and scepticism, Major Tom questions, "No man's land... The Germans... Are they not there? Have I somehow escaped the horrors of war? And my name is Tom, short for Thomas, and everybody calls me Major Tom." He begins to wonder if this is a dream of alternative reality.

Robin gently reassures Major Tom, "My dear Major, there are no Germans here, nor any signs of war." He continues, "You find yourself in a peaceful park, surrounded by nature's beauty."

Major Tom, gradually comprehending the situation, feels a mixture of gratitude and confusion, and mutters to himself, "How is it possible? Was it all a dream? Or have I truly been granted a respite from the atrocities of war, a chance to experience life's tranquillity once more?" The weight of his past experiences and the sudden contrast of his current surroundings overwhelm him, leaving him in a state of introspection and wonder.

Robin, perceptive to Major Tom's inner turmoil, offers his wisdom, "Sometimes our minds create illusions to shield us from harsh realities, perhaps this park, with its serene landscape, is the solace of your needs." He adds, "Embrace the tranquillity and allow it to heal your weary soul."

Major Tom takes a deep breath, allowing the peaceful ambiance to seep into his being. He decides to cherish this newfound sanctuary and find solace in the simplicity of Rozelle Park. The echoes of war fade into the background as Major Tom embraces the present moment, grateful for the respite from the horrors he has known. With each step, he walks further away from the burdens of his past, finding a renewed sense of hope inner peace amidst the serenity of Rozelle Park. Together with Robin, they revel in beauty of a Wee Loch, the gentle rustling of leaves, and the graceful flight of birds overhead. Major Tom finds solace in his newfound reality, knowing that peace, even if temporary, is a precious gift to be cherished.

Robin perches on a nearby branch, fluffing his feathers as he attempts to explain the extraordinary event that unfolded in Rozelle Park.

He speaks with excitement, "Recounting how, during the sunset, a rare alignment occurred." He talks of, "The eclipse of the sun cast a mesmerising glow over the horizon, illuminating the sky with vibrant colours of purples and oranges."

It was as if nature itself conspired to create a moment of tranquillity and healing for Major Tom. Then he continues, "As the sun disappears below the horizon, the Northern Lights emerges, dancing across the heavens with their fragile beauty. The green lights of the Aurora seem to reach down and warm up the Wee Loch, creating a magical energy that enveloped the entire park. The Wee Loch undergoes a magical transformation, turning into a serene pool enveloped in a shimmering mist of emerald, green.

This mist gradually expands, spreading its enchanting essence throughout Rozelle Park, infusing life into statues and the carvings scattered throughout. From the old oak tree to the majestic statue of Major Tom, every element comes to life, awakening from their once stationary existence."

Unbeknownst to Robin and Major Tom, the friendly neighbourhood squirrel, Peaches, is drawn to the commotion, and arrives at the scene.

Peaches, the inquisitive and agile squirrel, scampered over to join the conversation. She perched on a nearby branch, her ears twitching with curiosity as she listens to Robin and Major Tom exchange words.

Peaches cannot help but be intrigued by unfolding tale of the park's extraordinary transformation. With her tiny paws clutching to an acorn, she chatters excitedly, "I've seen the green lights and I felt the park come alive like nothing I've ever witnessed before." She goes on to say, "Tell me more about this! Robin, and what we should do next?"

Robin, delighted by Peaches' enthusiasm, continues to the narrative, sharing the interactions between the awakened statues. Major Tom, still astounded by the turn of events, eagerly engages in conversation with his newfound companions, fascinated by their perception of life during his carved existence.

As the trio, converses under the enchanting green glow, they discover the share longing for peace and harmony. They realise that despite their different forms and backgrounds, they all seek solace in the tranquillity of Rozelle Park, a sanctuary where the complexities of the world can be momentarily set aside.

Together, Robin, Major Tom, and Peaches embark on a journey of discovery, navigating the delicate balance between the real and the magical, as they embrace the unity forged in their extraordinary encounters. Little do they know that the park holds more surprises and adventures in store, inviting them to unravel the mysteries that lie beneath its serene façade.

Chapter six.

Major Tom's Battles:

His Memories Resurfaces.

Major Tom, having left Manchester behind, finds himself in amidst of a war against the Germans in France. Memories of his time on the battlefield floods his thoughts, recalling the hardships and struggles he faced during the conflict. The impact of his war experience weighs heavily on his mind, as he grabbles with fragmented memories that resurfaced. Amidst the chaos of battle, one memory stands out---the year 1917 in a place known as Ypres, known to the troops as "Wipers." The battles fought there, etched in his mind as the last clear recollection before everything becomes hazy. Now, in a strange twist of fate, a newspaper land on his lap, bearing the date 21/05/2023. This bewildered occurrence deepens his confusion, leaving him questioning he has entered the afterlife. Or some other unknown realm. Amidst the fog of his memories, Major Tom struggles to recall the names his loved ones, especially that of his wife, mother, and son he believes he had.

Manchester, the place he left behind, holds the fragments of his past life, urging him to unravel the mysteries with his own identity.

Robin turns to Peaches with anticipation, his eyes gleaming with curiosity. "Do you have any messages for me?" he asks eagerly.

Peaches, with her mischievous glint in her eye, nods, and replies, "I've got something for you, the tree surgeons recently carved a face into the Acorn that resides by me in the old oak tree." She adds, "Now Acorn can talk and I've a message passed on to you."

Robin feathers ruffled with excitement as he chirps, "A message from Acorn? How intriguing! What is the message?"

Peaches relays the message from Acorn to Robin, "Acorn urges you to establish communications with the rest of the statues and the carvings throughout Rozelle Park. He warns that without proper connections and the understanding in the park, there may be chaos."

Robin ponders the important of this message, realising that unity and cooperation among of the awakening park's residents are crucial to maintaining harmony.

With a newfound sense of purpose, Robin sets off on a mission to bridge the gap between the various statues and carvings, hoping to foster with an understanding and to create a peaceful coexistence within Rozelle Park.

Robina just swoops in, her wings fluttering gently as she lands beside Robin. She speaks with a touch of annoyance, "Robin, it is time to come home. I have just got the babies off to sleep."

Robin introduces Major Tom to Robina, his voice frills with enthusiasm, "Darling, meet Major Tom, he had quite of an adventure today."

Robina blushes, her feathers slightly ruffled, as she greets Major Tom with a warm smile, "Hello, Major Tom. It is a pleasure to meet you."

Peaches have been a busy squirrel, interrupts, "I've got a couple of tasks to do as well, and I got to speak to Nurse Gladys."

Major Tom, realising the need for practicality, spoke up, "Well, we cannot organise any tasks tonight. Let us leave them for tomorrow." He also asks, "Peaches, where can we find Nurse Gladys?"

Peaches pointing her tiny paw behind the back of Major Tom, and replies, "She's just a hundred yards behind you, Major Tom. You cannot miss her."

As the sun begins to set, casting a warm glow over Rozelle Park. The Robins make their way home, and Peaches heads off towards Nurse Gladys. Her voice fills with anticipation and a hint of mischief as she is preparing to embark on the next chapter of their enchanted adventures.

Chapter Seven.

Nurse Gladys Revelations:

Peaches Unveils the Awakening.

Although Peaches advances towards Nurse Gladys, she stands there on top of the tree post, just like Major Tom's. Nurse Gladys is dressed in a dark green army dress. Made of sturdy fabric with a brass buttons running down the front. The dress is long, reaching all the way down to her ankles, and has a slight flare at the bottom. She wears a white apron over her dress, with a Red Cross embroidered on the front. Indicating her role as a nurse. Her head is covered with white cap adorn with a red cross, and she wears a white bonnet tied around her neck. Over her shoulders, she dons a dark green cloak with red lining. which she can wrap around herself in case of wintry weather, or it is starts to rain.

Peaches explains to Nurse Gladys, "That she, the other statues and the carvings have been brought to life by a strange event occurred a few nights ago."

Nurse Gladys, feeling a bit confused asks Peaches, "Will she remember her family?"

Peaches realises that Nurse Gladys is still trapped in her old memories from when she was a real person and attempts to explain, "Now that you're a statue, you don't have a family, all the memories you have, aren't your own." Nurse Gladys becomes upset and starts to cry, but she comforts Nurse Gladys and says, "While you may not have a biological family, you now have a new family consisting of statues and the carvings in this park." Peaches reminds her with a message conveyed by Acorn, "We need for all statues to come together to establish communication to prevent chaos." Nurse Gladys begins to feel better and agrees to lend her assistance to the cause. Nurse Gladys confused and struggling to understand what Peaches is saying. She is certain that she is not a statue and vividly remembers being a nurse during the war.

However, she cannot recall her family, and her own age, which troubles her deeply. Peaches mentions something about the sun being blocked by the moon, causing an eclipse, and resulting in heighten solar flare activity interacting with the Northern Lights (Aurora Borealis), creating a radiant green light. This green light warms up the Wee Loch and releases a mist to spread over the park. Bringing the statues and the carvings to life. But to Nurse Gladys, it all feels like a dream, and she is not sure what is happening to her. She tries to make sense of Peaches' explanation. She wondered how it could be possible for the statues and the carvings to have memories of people who have died a long time ago.

Peaches reiterates, "When the tree surgeon selects a tree to be carved, they remove the branches and shape the sculpture based on their imagination. This time, they sculpted Nurse Gladys, a nurse from the bygone era." Peaches further explains to Nurse Gladys, "The statues and the carvings have absorbed the memories of the individuals they represent." However, this information remains perplexing for Nurse Gladys. Despite the confusion, she strives to comprehend and find meaning of it all.

Chapter Eight:

Plans for Tomorrow.

Martin Overhears.

The Girls Chatting Below.

As the girls continue with their gossiping, A House Martin suddenly swoops overhead, capturing his attention. He notices something strange happening down below and decides to investigate. With swift and precise flight, he descends and lands on Nurse Gladys shoulder, seeking a closer look and then introducing himself as, "Martin." Peaches informs him about their mission to spread the word and to establish communications with the animals in Rozelle Park.

However, Martin is preoccupied with the task of finding insects to feed his family. He explains, "My partner Martina is currently sitting on her chicks to keep them warm. I must embark on a search for insects to feed or else I risk losing them."

House Martins have two broods of eggs each season, like the Robins. The survival of the offspring's is crucial for the continuation of their species. House Martins are known for their unique nesting habits. They build the nests on the outside walls of the buildings under the eaves. They can also be found nesting inside the roofs or the sheds. House Martins are colonial nesters, and they have an average nest size of four to five eggs, The eggs are white and laid at a daily interval. However, severe weather sometimes can delay, the laying process. Severe weather can seriously affect the growth and the survival of House Martins chicks because the rely on the flying insects for food. The female of the species, Incubates the eggs for about a week until they hatch, because the chicks are born without feathers, and then the females must keep them warm for a week until their feathers have grown. The chicks typically leave the nest after 22 to 23 days, depending on the size of the brood and the weather. After leaving their nests, the young House Martins returns to roost and nourish for several days before dispersing for migration.

Peaches looks up at Martin with a pleading eye, "Can you help us?" She asks, her eyes fill with hope.

Martin pauses for a minute. Considering the request. Finally, he replies with a spark of determination in his eyes, "Yes, I think I can. Us Martins lives together in a bustling colony. I can ask the boys for some assistance."

A glimmer of relief shines on Peaches' face, "That would be wonderful," she says gratefully. "But where's your colony located?"

"Our colony!" Martin explains curiosity brimming in his voice. "It resides just beyond Rozelle Park gates, nestled within an aged cottage that we proudly call home. The front wall, adorned with our colonial friends under the old guttering, provides a perfect sanctuary for us. The surrounding woods teem with insects, and I have spent an entire day hunting them down. That is how I happened to fly over your heads and overhear your conversation, prompting me to descend and investigate."

Peaches nods, with the understanding of this situation. "During the day, there's no more danger from the statues inhabiting the park." She reassures Martin. "They remain in a state of hibernation, allowing you to raise your precious chicks without worrying. Only when the sun descends, and the public retreats, around about 8 30 PM, that when the statues awaken, and we can carry messages throughout Rozelle Park swiftly and unseen. And once we have fulfilled our duty, we can all return home and rest."

Martins wings flutter with anticipation. "Can we start this mission today?" He asks eagerly.

Peaches shakes her little head gently. "Not today," she replies with a touch of disappointment in her voice. "We are waiting for the arrival of Robin. He believes tomorrow will be the better time, as today has been quite hectic for him. He needs to return to his nest to find some solace and rest."

Martin nods understandingly, his weariness starting to show. "Very well," he says. "I suppose, I need some rest too. I will gather up all my friends, and we will meet you tomorrow." Eager to determine the meeting's location, Martin inquires. "Where should we gather?"

Peaches points in the direction of Major Tom's Post, indicating its visibility from their current location. "You can see his post from here," she says, her gaze shifting to a particular statue. "That's the one catches Nurse Gladys eye." Nurse Gladys voice pitches higher than usual, her cheeks blushing with a reddish glow. "Peaches!" she bellows, unable to contain her surprise. Peaches cannot help but smile in response to the unexpected encounter.

In a friendly exchange, Martin concludes, "Alright then, I am glad. I am feeling a bit fatigue myself, so I must hurry back to my nest." He adds, "I will call on my friends tomorrow. See you then!" With that, they bid each other farewell, their aspirations intertwined as they prepare for the adventure that waits for them tomorrow.

Peaches observes the two statues, her eyes filling with curiosity. "I see, there are two more statues behind you, moving about 50 yards from here." She says, pointing towards them. "One is kneeling, holding what looks a rifle in his right hand, as if he is in a prayer. The other soldier is lying on what look a stretcher, his right hand covering a wound. Are they the ones you mentioned before, Nurse Gladys?"

Nurse Gladys nods solemnly. "Yes, you describe them accurately," she replies, her voice carrying a tinge of sadness. "My memories of these statues hold the lives of lost souls. Recollections become intertwined with their own being. The soldier kneeling is known as Sergeant Lee, bearing an injury on his upper left arm. The second soldier's name is Gunner Peterson. He was critically wounded in his chest and lies there on a stretcher. From what I can recall, I tended their wounds yesterday.

Gunner Peterson was not able to overcome his injuries, so I am presuming they have already passed away. Their souls, like mine, were missing, and somehow, the statues have absorbed their souls." A sense of sadness hangs into the air as the girls contemplate the fate of these fallen soldiers, forever carved into wood.

Chapter Nine:

The Foot Soldiers.

Arrival in the Afterlife.

The Manchester Regiment soldiers don a distinct uniform that speaks of their bravery and commitment. Adorned in deep shade of khaki, their jackets boast a sturdy fabric, meticulously tailored to withstand the rigours of battle. The emblem of the Manchester Regiment is intricately embroidered on their chest, symbolising their unwavering loyalty. Their trousers, crisply pressed, bear the mark of discipline and unity. Black leather boots, polished to a gleaming shine, march steadfastly across the terrain. Their headgear, a fusion of particularly and tradition, crowns them with dignity. The Manchester Regiment uniform encapsulates their indomitable spirit and dedication to their noble cause.

The Manchester Regiment soldiers are armed with the iconic Lee Enfield rifle, a-bolt action repeating rifle. It held significant important as a primary firearm of the British Empire and the Commonwealth armed forces during the first half of the 20th century. Serving as a standard rifle for the British armies, from its official adoption in 1895 until 1957, in reference, the version used during that period is often referred to the SMLE, which stands for Short Magazine Lee Enfield. It is design and reliability made it a notable weapon throughout the various conflicts of that era.

Gratefully for Nurse Gladys offers valuable insights as Peaches expresses her appreciation. "I thank you for sharing their names and granting me the opportunity to deliver the message to them." She speaks. "I must proceed on my way now, and I'll see you tomorrow." With determination, Peaches embarks towards the statues to fulfil her mission.

Nurse Gladys bids farewell with a warm smile, replying, "Cheerio." With her voice resonates with gratitude and hope. As Peaches ventures off towards the soldiers. Nurse Gladys watches her departure, her thoughts lingering on the extraordinary journey that lies ahead.

Engulfed in a sea of contemplation, Sergeant Lee finds himself adrift in a cascade of thoughts. With a relevant hush, he begins to recite a heartfelt prayer, fervently seeking solace and drawing upon the wellspring of strength within him.

Each word spills forth, resonating with a deep yearning for guidance and resilience. In the stillness of the moment, surrounded by the echoes of his whisper's entreaties, Sergeant Lee finds solace in a sacred embrace of his prayer, knowing that it will be his steadfast companion through the trials that lie ahead.

Our Father, who art in heaven,

Hallowed be thy name.

Thy kingdom come.

Thy will be done,

On earth as it is in heaven.

Give us this daily bread.

And forgive us our trespasses,

As we forgive those who trespass against us.

And lead us not into temptation,

But deliver us from evil.

For thine is the kingdom,

The power, and the glory,

Forever and ever.

Amen.

Turning his attention to Gunner Peterson, Sergeant Lee speaks with a mix of concern and encouragement. "Well, mate, I must make my way and report back to the front. Tomorrow we will be going over the top. Stay strong, my friend. You will be back in Blighty in no time, you lucky chap!"

Out of nowhere, Peaches emerges, instantly capturing his focus as she rushes to interrupts, yelling, "Hold on! Just a moment! You are not going anywhere. Both you and Gunner Peterson have been transformed into living statues by the tree surgeons, forever incorporated within the very essence of a magnificent trees."

Sergeant Lee's face reflects a mix of bewilderment and confusion as his brows furrow, questioning, "What do you mean, statues? I have been consoling my companion for hours as he nears the end, and now you share this news. Furthermore, he exclaims, "Goodness gracious! I find myself Conversing with a squirrel!"

Peaches nods understandably confused. "Yes, you are not dreaming, and I am a squirrel. Now, I want you to check your wounds. Look at your left arm and examine Gunner Peterson's wounds as well. Also, search for any scars that may be visible." Sergeant Lee, filled with curiosity and disbelief, decides to inspect his carved body for any signs of wounds. With a mixture of anticipation, and trepidation, he carefully examines the wooden service, running his hand all over it. He searches for any hints of scars or injuries, as his fingers tracing the contours of his body. Suddenly, his eyes widen with surprise. "There it is!" he whispers, noticing a faint marking on his left arm "A scar.... I carry the remnants of my past, even in this statue form."

A wave of an astonishment washes over him as he ponders to implications. The connections between his former self and his current state seems undeniable, as it is a tangible link. Turning his attention to Gunner Peterson, he is eager to examine the statue for any similar traces of wounds. He yearns to uncover more clues about their shared history, hoping that the answers they seek are waiting to be discovered within these statues.

Sergeant Lee looks at Peaches with a mixture of confusion and hope shining in his eyes. "Is Gunner Peterson truly dead?" He asks, seeking some clarification.

Peaches gently shakes her tiny head. "No, he is not. His memories of his passing have carried over to his existence. You both now in the afterlife."

Understanding began to be drawn on Sergeant Lee as he absorbs his added information. "So, Gunner Peterson is merely asleep?" He asks, seeking confirmation.

Peaches nods reassuringly, her small body filled with a sense of assurance. "Yes, that is right. He is in a state of sleep. All you need to do is give him a firm slap, and he will wake up."

Determined to reunite with his comrade, Sergeant Lee urgently raises his right hand and delivers a couple of gentle slaps to Gunner Peterson's statue form. The sound echoes through the stillness, with anticipation filling the air as they wait for a response. They hope that Sergeant Lee actions will rouse Gunner Peterson from his dormant state.

Gunner Peterson, Still feeling disoriented, regains consciousness with a sensation akin to being struck by a massive force. He exclaims, "What happened? I feel like a ton of bricks fell on me."

Sergeant Lee stands there, dumbfounded yet overjoyed, unable to believe his eyes. He whispered in disbelief. "Oh my god, he is alive. I cannot believe it. It is as if he came back from the dead."

Gunner Peterson, in a state of confusion, questions, the situation, asking, "What do you mean? I come back from the dead?"

Peaches, raising her voice to interrupt the conversation, inserts herself, determined to provide an explanation. "Stop! I must intervene and try to explain what is happening here."

Gunner Peterson, bewildered by the spectacle of a talking squirrel, then mutters to himself. "I must be dead if a squirrel is talking to me."

Peaches quickly clarifies. "No, you are not dead. And yes, you are indeed talking to a squirrel. My name is Peaches, and I am here to tell you a particular story." She proceeds to recount the events of the past few nights, shedding a light on their current predicaments. She continued. "Both of you were carved by the tree surgeons from trunks of an old trees. One of those trees has fallen. And that tree is you, Gunner Peterson! The memories you possess do not belong to you. They are the memories of a lost soul."

Gunner Peterson puzzled and asked, "So, this is a recollection of my girlfriend, my mother, and my family.... they are not my own, but memories of a lost soul."

Peaches affirms, "Yes, exactly. Nurse Gladys came to the same conclusion amidst these strange happenings. However, we still cannot explain why the statues and the carvings have come to life or why we, as living animals, have gained ability to speak?"

Sergeant Lee, feeling the sense of urgency, asks, "What can we do about this?"

Peaches concludes, "I have a friend named Robin who is currently working on finding a solution to this problem. But for now, we must wait until tomorrow and hear the reports from Major Tom. I hope that Robin will have an answer. So, I bid you goodbye for now." With that, Peaches makes her way home, her energy is now waning. The two soldiers bid farewell, expressing their gratitude for her insights, and hoping for the resolution of their peculiar circumstances.

Chapter Ten:

Robins Feeding Their Young.

Robin and His Boys Meet the Martins.

The following morning, a gentle Scottish mist begins to form over the Wee Loch. As the mist slowly covers the surrounding area, Robin gazes upwards, greeting by a breath-taking sight. Against the backdrop of a brilliant blue sky, two commercial airliners streaked across the sky, leaving behind water vapour trails that intersect to form a striking white cross. It resembles an ironic representation of the Scottish flag, proudly fluttering in the vast expanse of the sky. Robin stirs by the beauty of the moment, turns to his attention to the nest. The air fills with the insistent chirping of their hungry hatchlings, their tiny voices pleading for nourishment. "Feed us, Mummy, Daddy! We are hungry!" they are all yelling in unison; their hunger is now palpable.

In these early days, the hatchlings appear larger than their own parents, a result of their continuous growth during the first two weeks of their lives. Weight gains is crucial during this period, as it prepares them for the challenges that lay ahead.

However, now's the time for them to venture beyond the confines of their warm nest, to explore, exercise, shed their extra weight, learn to fly, and then embark on the remarkable journey of migration.

As the Robins scour the area in search of sustenance, the hatchlings observe intently, and their curiosity piqued. They absorb every moment, every action on their parents, as if imprinted with the wisdom of the generations past. Fluttering clumsily on nearby branches, they attempt to mimic the graceful manoeuvres of their experienced parents, their determination shines through their efforts.

Under the watchful guidance of their parents, the hatchlings gradually gain strength. Refining their flight skills and becoming proficient in finding food. They understand that their journey is not solely about satisfying their own hunger, but also about being a part of a larger tapestry of life. That they are destined to migrate, to seek new lands, and contributing to the cycle of life in their own unique way.

Through this process, the hatchlings not only shed their excess weight but also develop a deep connection with their natural surroundings. As the day passes and the hatchlings grow stronger, their bond with their parents deepens. Together, they forged a united front, ready to face the challenges and wonders that await them during their upcoming migration.

With each passing moment, the hatchlings gain the confidence and resilience needed to embark on this transformative journey. And so, against the backdrop of the misty Scottish morning. Robin and his family prepare to take flight. Their wings, fuelled by determination and love, carry them forward into the vast expanse of Rozelle Park, where they will join the symphony of migratory birds and leave their mark on the tapestry of nature.

Robin approaches his partner, Robina, with a gentle tone, his voice filled with concern and affection. "Robina, my darling, let's sit down and talk about what has transpired yesterday evening."

Robina, still harbouring with some resentment, replies curtly, "What are we going to do about it? I am still angry with you. You left me alone, responsible for bringing our precious baby's home."

Robina anger softens slightly as she listens to Robin's remorseful voice. "What is it that you need to discuss with the House Martins?" she asks, her tone tingled with frustration.

Robin takes a deep breath, his voice filled with sincerity. "I need to seek their help for the well-being of Rozelle Park. If I cannot find an assistance, the park could descend into chaos. The House Martins' females are currently occupied with caring for their featherless chicks, which is a responsibility that will last for a week. During this time, the males will have some free time."

However, Robina remains unconvinced, her voice tinged with a sadness, "So, you're just going to leave me alone again?" She sniffs. Robin pauses for a moment. Contemplating on the situation, and he speaks gently. "Yes, but I will take a couple of hatchlings with me and feed them along the way. They need nourishment and exercise too. you can stay here if you want, tending to our nest with the girls! I will take the boys with me as we make our way to the House Martins colonies."

Robina sighs, her feathers ruffles with mixed emotions. She understands the importance of Robin's mission and he need to look for an assistance, but the thought of being left behind still weighs heavily on her heart. Deep down, she knows Robin's intentions are noble, driven by a desire to ensure the harmony of Rozelle Park and the well-being of their avian companions. Reluctantly, she nods, her voice filled with resignation. "I suppose it is necessary for you to go but promise me you will take loving care of our hatchlings and return them safely. They are our precious ones."

Robin's gaze softens with his deep love for Robina and their family, as he speaks with tender reassurance, "I promise to you, my dear. I will watch over them and bring them back to you safely, stronger than ever before. Go on, enjoy some quality time with your daughters. And when we reunite, we will continue our journey as a united flock."

Robin and his sons embark on their aerial journeys, gracefully soaring through the sky towards House Martin's, nest by the cottage just outside of Rozelle Park. As they draw closer, they observe a flurry of activity around the bustling colonies.

Among the House Martins, Martina bears a great responsibility, diligently keeping her chicks warm as Martin fulfils his nurturing role. The present time places an additional burden on Martin, as he tirelessly searches for insects to nourish his growing family. Fortunately, favourable weather conditions have resulted in an abundance of insects swirling around the colony, providing ample substance for the chicks' growth under the protective cover of the cottage's roof guttering.

Four additional broods of House Martins' chicks have also established their nests nearby, presenting a potential source of assistance for Robin's endeavours. As the sun begins its descent, the diminishing availability of insects' grants Martin some spare time on his hands. He welcomes the opportunity to take a break from constant hunting and engaging in different activities, savouring a momentary respite.

Martin arrives at his nest, greeted by the hungry cries of his chicks. "Daddy, Daddy, we are hungry! Feed me first!"

Martin understands the hierarchy of his family. The loudest and most in insistent chick is deemed to be the hungriest and receives the food first, while Martina is fed last. Martin recognises the importance of nourishing Martina, as her well-being is essential for their shared life and future endeavours. Robin and his son's lands near Martin's nest, relieved to see that all the Martin's chicks are thriving, and none have been lost.

Martina's devoted care has ensured their warmth and well-being. Robin cannot help but express his amusement, saying, "I see you still have five chicks! Have you named them yet?"

Martin replies with a hint of a caution. "No, we have not. It is too soon. We might lose one or two and besides, Martina will have the honour of naming them."

Sensing the opportunity, Robin then reveals his purpose, saying, "I'm here to ask the favour from you." Martin inquires, "Is it about what happened last night?"

Robin confirms, "Yes, it is."

Martin nods, sharing of his knowledge. "I have met Peaches, and she informs me about your mission. What favour do you seek from me? And may I ask, what names have you given to your little ones? I see they already taken their first flight from the Nest."

Robin proudly shared his boy's names, saying, "My boys are known as James and Elvis. They are now over thirteen days old, and my boys follows me throughout the day." Eager to address the favour, Robin continues, "I need to ask a question. Once the park closes and the statues awakens, there will be great uncertainty unfolds. The other evening, I went to investigate a statue carved from a tree stump, a silhouette of a soldier."

Martin interrupt's, "Major Tom."

Robin smiles, with acknowledging Peaches involvement, "So, Peaches have told you then."

Martin confirms, "Yes, she did."

Robin perceives to recount his conversation with Major Tom expressing his surprise. "He still believes he is a man, even though Peaches told him he is a statue with the memories of the soul that his wooden body absorbed. The story continues. And then Peaches appears, revealing that a tree surgeons decided to carve a face into an Acorn which miraculously started to speak. Acorn's purpose was to gather many animals as possible and spread the message throughout Rozelle Park.

The message was to inform the statues that are no longer mere soldiers but become a living character with the memories of their lost soul."

Martina, concerning about the situation, she asks." What do we need to do?"

Martin reassures her, by saying, "There's nothing you can do that now, my dear. Your priority is to keep the chicks warm and safe."

Robin responds to Martin, saying, "I will need you around 8 30 tonight, just as the sun begins to set and the park closes and meet me by Major Tom's post. Can you gather more helpers?"

Martin nods and replies. "I will do my absolute best; I will ask my neighbours for assistance. Thank you, Robin!" By that time, insects have become scarce.

Martin flies back to his nest, making calls to his neighbours along the way, seeking for their assistance for upcoming mission. Meanwhile, Robin also returning to his nest, continue to feed his boys as he contemplates the arrangement for the evening and wonders who will be present. He notices some statues across Wee Loch, appearing as a team with pointy helmets curiously piqued, he decides to investigate them later in the evening, but for now, he must focus on feeding his boys. As Robin nears to his nest, he spots Robina have been enjoying some quality time with Nikki and Tina.

An idea has sparked his mind------what if the entire family goes to Major Tom's post for an evening out? This way, Robina can be present too, can listen to the plans for the mission.

Robin, with excitement of his voice, shares his idea with Robina, "Darling, I have a brilliant idea that just came to me. What if we all go out together as a family, taking our little ones with us? We can feed them along the way to Major Tom's Post, and you might even hear the evening mission schedule first hand."

Robina's eyes light up as she responds. "What a wonderful idea! It would be a great family outing." Meanwhile, Martin has successfully reached out to his neighbours, sharing the good news. They have accepted the invitation and eager to join him. It turns out there will be four additional helping hands.

The neighbours of the Martins have received permission from their partners to go on a mission with him. Filled with joy, Martin soars back to his nest, confident that Robin's plan will bring happiness to all those involved in Rozelle Park.

Chapter eleven:

Return to the Old Oak Tree.

The Arrival of Woody and Doodle.

Rozelle Park closes at its regular time of 8 30, prompting the Robins to gather all their offspring's and fly towards Major Tom's post. At the same time, the male House Martins commence on their journey. Suddenly, the Hands pocket watch alarm goes off, it vibrates sending shivers throughout Rozelle Park, awakening all the statues and the carvings.

Peaches abandons her dray and approaches Acorn with joyful expression, eager to share good news. "Acorn," she calls, "I have exciting news for you! Robin and I, we are planning to make our way to Major Tom's Post this evening. Our goal is to coordinate a mission that will avert any potential chaos in this park, and we need to start tonight."

Acorn responds with a mixed relief and concern, saying, "That's good to hear. But I also have a message for you to deliver regarding the statues."

Intrigued, Peaches asks, "What is the message?"

Acorn sends the message to Peaches, informing her that the statues can detach themselves from their posts. Acorn instructs Peaches to pass the message to Major Tom and swiftly heads towards Major Tom's location. Just as Peaches leaves, another squirrel named Doodle appears.

Barney extends a warm welcome to Doodle expressing, "T' wit, T' woos, T' wit, T' woos." He further says, "Welcome stranger!" The other carvings join in with a friendly greeting, "Hi." Barney proceeds to inquire, "T' wit, T' woos, T' wit, T' woos." He also adds, "May I know your name?"

Doodle introduces himself with a friendly smile, saying, "Doodle."

Lefty face curiously asks, "Why have you come to this tree? "

Doodle replies, "I'm actually looking for Peaches."

Righty face informs him. "You just missed her." He further adds, "She's currently on a mission."

Patiently, Doodle responds. "Oh, I see! Well, can I wait here for her?"

Barney offers reassurance, saying, "T' wit, T' woos, T' wit, T' woos." He further adds, "of course, you can!"

Doodle then mentions. "I heard Peaches is looking for a partner to raise her next season's litter. "

Righty face expresses slightly confused and admits, "We don't have any clues regarding whether she's seeking a partner." Doodle nods, acknowledging the given information.

Acorn offers a suggestion, saying, "I suggest you go and wait for Peaches' in her dray until she returns from her mission."

Curiously, Doodle asks, "Where can I find it?"

Acorn replies, "It is at the top of the tree, next to Barney's perch. You can wait for her there."

Doodle, a lively squirrel, swiftly ascends the tree trunk, overtaking Barney, and leaps into the Dray, eagerly waiting for Peaches. Just then, Woody, enters the vicinity, completely unaware of Barney presence. In an unfortunate turn of events, Woody collides with Barney, causing both to stumble. Woody attempts to regain his flight, flounders and eventually crashes to the ground. Woody cries with a "Ouch!"

Barney, a combination of surprise and annoyance, bellows, "T' wit, T' woos, T' wit, T' woos. He shouts, "Watch where you're going!"

Woody feeling slightly flustered, apologises. "I am so sorry! I did not see you there." He then adds, "My eyesight isn't the best in low light conditions."

Barney, gently caresses his wooden surface and he responds, "T' wit, T' woos, T' wit, T' woos." He continues, "Well, kindly exercise more caution in the future. You nearly dislodged me from my perch!"

Woody, a wooden wood pigeon with remarkable ability to fly, sheepishly nods, fully aware of his mistake, and pledges to be more thoughtful next time. With the incident behind them, they both find their calm and resume cherishing the remainder of the evening in the tranquillity of the tree.

Lefty faced Chimes in. "By the way, what is your name?"

Woody replies, "I'm Woody."

Righty face points towards a spot behind Barney, gesturing for Woody to find a perch there, "You can stay there for a while, just try not to disturb Barney. We are now enjoying the quiet." Righty face advises. Woody nods gratefully and settles down vowing to keep the peace and avoid for any further mishaps.

Acorn steps forward, but his voice fills with conviction. "Friends and companions, I stand before you today to address the pressing matters that have unfolded in Rozelle Park. This old oak tree has witnessed an influx of visitors and attention, and now it is our collective responsibility ensure that the preservation of its harmony and the beauty.

Considering recent events, we find ourselves faced with a crucial mission. Our dear friends and guardian, Major Tom, remains unaware of his current state of the statue with the memories of Lost Souls.

Peaches, the courageous squirrel, has brought this to our attention, urging us to bring clarity and tranquillity to Major Tom's existence. Together with our variant Robin's allies. Robin shall embark on a journey to Major Toms Post.

As twilight descends and the park closes, awakening all statues and the carvings, we will seize these mystical moments to communicate and the enlightenment of Rozelle Park. Our purpose is clear: We must convey a measurement of messages that they are no longer soldiers bound by duty, but rather guardians of this park, its stories, and their memories.

Major Tom must understand all their transform state for their own well-being and the prosperity of our cherished park. I plead to each one of you, be your statues, carvings, birds, or any other animals, to join us in a crucial endeavour.

Unite your presence in support, for it is through our collective strengths that we can forge a future where the statues and the carvings are no longer lost souls, but rather enlightenment guardians embodying the wisdom and tails of our park. Let us ally with our spirits to raise voices, embrace our overwhelming determination.

As darkness descends upon the park and the Moon illuminates our path, let us embark on this journey of awakening and unity. The right time become to unlock Major Tom's true essence and restore equilibrium to our beloved home. May the light of hope to guide our way, and may our action shape the destiny of the hallowed land we call home."

Acorn resounding words fills the air, instantly renewed sense of purpose and the unity among the gathering of statues, carvings and birds, animals with our hearts ablaze and determined kindles with and they prepare themselves for the task that lies ahead, ready to embark on a journey that hold the key to Major Toms enlightenment and the restoration of Rozelle Park's harmonious existence.

Chapter Twelve:

Establishing Communications.

Arrival of the Feathery Messengers.

Amidst the turbulence of World War One, effective communications emerged as a pivotal factor in military operations. Major Tom, immovable like a statue at his post, found himself facing a predicament.

Bereft of access to modern communication methods, he was confined to the verbal exchanges, an arduous task given his inability to move. Yet, he comprehended the significance of relaying crucial information to his comrades. Contemplating his options, Major Tom delved into various methods of communication available during the war.

While verbal communication seems the obvious, it is requirement for proximity rendered it unfeasible in his present circumstances. He could not abandon his post to personally deliver messages over the long distances.

Other methods came to mind, such as semaphore, a system of using flags to convey messages over long distance. However, Major Tom lacked the necessary equipment and assistance for such a method.

Another well-known communication method was Morse Code, a system utilising dots and dashes to represent letters and numbers, widely employed in military operation with proven effectiveness. Unfortunately, Major Tom lacked the means to transmit Morse Code messages from his position.

Similarly, the highly effective telephone system remained beyond his reach, leaving him yearning for the ability to connect with his fellow soldiers by simply picking up a receiver. Alas, it remained unattainable.

Considering this, Major Tom turned his attention to Pigeons, renowned for their innate homing instincts and their capacity to effectively communicate messages. However, their reliable on freedom to fly back to their intended destinations made them unsuitable for his current circumstances.

Lastly, Major Tom considered a simple, yet impractical method often employed by children, a piece of string with two tin cans attached to each end. Frustrated by the limitations imposed upon him, he understood the imperative of finding a mean to communicate despite his stationary position.

Verbal communications remained his sole option, and he fervently hoped for the return of Robin and his companions to his post, mentally preparing himself to seize any opportunity for dialogue that might arise.

Aware of the challenges, Major Tom recognises his critical role in the larger mission, and his unwavering commitment to fulfil his duty burning fiercely within him. Standing watchfully at his post, his gaze caught sight of a familiar group approaching the Robins, accompanied by their newfound allies and friends, an ample number of assistants to aid in his mission. Renowned for their resourcefulness and determination, the Robins had proven themselves to be reliable allies. Major Tom eagerly awaits their arrival, hoping that they would bring with them the means to establish the much-needed verbal communications he desperately sought.

Major Tom's excitement grew as he sees the Robins and their friends approaching him. He cannot contain his joy and exclaims, "I'm thrilled to see you all here!"

The hatchlings, hungry and impatient, crying out, "Feed Me. Feed Me, we're hungry!"

Robin turns to his dearest Robina and demands, "This meeting is crucial for us to set up communications. Can you carry on feeding, the young ones? I must listen to this meeting."

Robina, torn between her desires and to listen and her duty as a mother, responds with a sniffle, "I want to listen to the meeting too. but the babies need me."

Sunny, a friend of Martin, offers his assistance saying, "Let me help feed the babies so that you can listen to the meeting, Robina."

Grateful for the offer, Robina replies, "Thank you, Sunny. That is a generous offer. After the meeting, when Robin wraps up and goes on his own way, you can help me feed the babies on the way back to my nest." She introduces her Hatchlings to Sunny, saying, "This is James, Elvis and Nikki and Tina."

With the babies in capable hands, Robina feels a sense of relief and anticipation as she prepares to join the important meeting and she is eager to continue with the establishment of vital communications among Rozelle Park inhabitants.

Chapter Thirteen:

Peaches' Arrival.

A Liberation Unveils.

As the meeting commences, everyone's attention turns towards Major Tom, as they all wait for his orders. Just then, a rustling sound's catches their attention and Peaches emerges, darting towards Major Tom's post. With a sense of urgency, she announces, "I bring some news! Acorn informs me that the statues across the Wee Loch are planning to do something significant. We must unite all the statues and spread the message of peace throughout Rozelle Park. We must act swiftly or there will be chaos."

Her words send a shiver through the flock of birds, igniting a newfound determination to protect their homes and restore harmony.

But Major Tom asks, "But what about the statues and their plans? How does it relate to our role here?"

Peaches with serious expression, responds, "The statues aim to disrupt the harmony of Rozelle Park, but as long as we remain steadfast at our post during the day, we can ensure the effort is not in vain. Our presence and the recharging from your post are crucial to maintaining the balance and protecting our essence. Together, we can thwart their intentions and safeguard Rozelle Park."

The gravity of the situation weighs heavily on their minds as they prepare to face impending challenges. "Yes, that's why the message must be passed on." Peaches replies and goes on to say, "Acorn means that there will be chaos in Rozelle Park if you fail to stay at your posts."

Major Tom takes notice of these instructions and then asks, "You say if we don't get back to our post?" And he questions further, "How can I detach myself from my post?"

Peaches encourages him saying, "Go ahead and try."

Major Tom cautiously lifts his left foot first, feeling slightly bit sticky, then carefully places his foot on the ground. He repeats the same procedure with his right foot. With a smile, he yells, "It's easy, I have just detached myself, now I'm free!"

Robin asks a question, "This morning while I am flying from Martin's nest to mine, I notice statues with pointy helmets. Are they the Germans?"

Major Tom solemnly responds, "Yes, they are our enemies during the war, but now it is all over. I must pass on the message."

Martin Interrupts, "Do they know that?"

Major Tom gazes at Martin and admits, "Yeah, I'd like to say no, but I'm not sure."

Robin turns to Major Tom and asks, "What are the orders?"

Major Tom asserts, "The only way we can do this is through verbal communication, spreading the message across Rozelle Park to all the statues and carvings."

Major Tom's decision to rely on verbal communication poses both challenges and advantages. While it eliminates the need for complex equipment and specialised training. It also means that the accuracy and effectiveness of the messages depend on the clarity and reliability of the individuals involved.

The statues and the carvings diligently listen and accurately transmit the information as they receive it, ensuring that important messages are delivered without distortion or misinterpretation. The success of the communication system hinges on the trust and attentiveness of each participant, creating a sense of unity and shared responsibility within Rozelle Park's vibrant community.

Despite Its limitations, Major Tom remains hopeful that this simplified, yet essential form of communication will help them navigate the perils of war and safeguard this cherished park.

Major Tom instructs Robin and his Martin's friends to fly across the Wee Loch and convey to the Germans that the war is over. Then Major Tom and Peaches proceed towards Nurse Gladys. Meanwhile, Robina and her young hatchlings, as well as Sunny, fly back to Robina's nest, feeding them along the way.

Later, Major Tom and Peaches arrive at Nurse Gladys post "Hello, both of you," Nurse Gladys greets them. "Major Tom, how did you detach yourself from your post?"

Major Tom ponders for a moment. "Well, Peaches told me that we can all detach ourselves from our post. It goes like this: one leg forward and then the other leg."

Nurse Gladys attempts to follow the instructions but finds herself unable to move. Frustrated, she nervously shouts, "Major Tom, I cannot do it! How can I get loose?"

Major Tom shrugs and says, "I don't know, it just happens!" He adds, looking at Peaches, "Any ideas?"

Peaches contemplates the situation, "It is a matter of self-consciousness. When you become that person, you move unconsciously, influenced by the souls that you've absorb." Peaches then explains a little more, "Maybe, you can try to fully embody that person."

Nurse Gladys' makes several more attempts, each one filled with determination. After an hour of effort, a sudden force on her left leg results in a satisfying pop, finally, her leg is freed. She then focuses on the other leg, with a final push, she breaks free from her post. "Aaaaha ha! Aaaaha ha! I am finally managed to do it, I am free!" She shouts with her delight.

Peaches strikes on realisation, understood the underlying issue when encountering the statues. "It is crucial that they still believe they are the person they have become, "She explains. "Only then can they break away from their posts. We need to inform them that they are statues and the memories they possess do not belong to them." Peaches also become concerned about Robin and his friends facing the same challenge. She hopes that Robin will find a solution.

Major Tom, Peaches and Nurse Gladys gather, ready to discuss the important matter at hand. Peaches' eyes sparkle with amputation as she addresses the group, "I have something to share with all of you."

Major Tom leans in, his curiosity piqued, and asks, "What is it, Peaches? We are listening carefully."

Taking a deep breath, Peaches reveals, "This information is particularly relevant to all of you. You must remain at your post throughout the day, starting from sunrise until the alarm goes off before 8:30 AM, and continue until the park shuts at 8:30 PM.

During this time, your posts become a recharging point, it will nourish you and provide the energy you need during the night." Nurse Gladys raises her wooden eyebrow, seeking clarification. "So, we can recharge ourselves during Rozelle Park daylight hours. That is interesting."

Peaches nods her tiny head, her ear twitching, as she adds, "Exactly. It is crucial for your well-being. However, once the park shuts, you are free to detach yourself from your posts and explore Rozelle Park. But remember, you must return to your post before 8:30 AM in the morning." She continues, "Failure to return to your post currently results in your wooden materials igniting and turning you into ashes. The souls you have absorbed will be lost forever."

Nurse Gladys, filled with determination, responded, "Come along, Major Tom darling, and Peaches, let's go and find Sergeant Lee, and Gunner Peterson."

Peaches shouts, "Let's go!"

Major Tom eagerly replies, "Show me the way!" And together they set off towards the two soldiers ready to confront the next obstacle in their mission.

Chapter Fourteen:

Robina's Family Returns.

Bathed in Moonlight.

A homecoming.

They arrive at Robina's family home. Robina cannot help but feel a tinge of sadness as she listens to the rest of the meeting before heading off home. She wonders what Robin is doing at that moment, longing for his presence. Sensing her sadness, Sunny gently approaches her. "I bid you farewell, Robina," he says with a warm smile, "I need to check on my partner Cher and her chicks."

Robina musters a small smile in return, grateful for Sunny's company and assistance. "Thank you for everything," she says as Sunny takes off into the night sky, disappearing into the distance. Robina turns her attention back to her hatchlings, who are eagerly snuggled up against her. "Now, my little ones, it's time to rest," She coos lovingly. "Nikki. My sleepy darling, close your eyes. All the exercise today has made you tired."

Nikki let out a small yawn and nestled closer to Robina. "I'm sleepy, Mummy," She mumbled, with her eyes growing heavy.

Robina gently strokes Nikki's feathers by smoothing them out. "There now, my sweet. Close your eyes and close your eyes and so, you can drift off to sleep." One by one, her hatchlings follow suit, snuggling closely to their mother's warmth.

As the moon rises high in the night sky, casting a soft glow over their nest, Robina holds her precious babies even closer, feeling a deep sense of love and contentment. In this peaceful moment, she knows that they are safe and embraced by love of their family.

With a sign of relief, Robina settles down, her feathers gently covering her hatchlings. Sleep beckons, and one by one they drift off, their dreams and filled with wonders of Roselle Park.

Chapter Fifteen:

. A Multicultural Encounter.

Robin's Linguistical Adventure.

Let us start by observing the German soldiers who wore meticulously designed uniforms during the First World War. These uniforms convey a perfect balance of functionality and intimidation. The uniform consists of field-grey tunic and trousers, tailored for durability with the ease of movement on the battlefield.

The tunic features the soldier straps decorated with rank Insignia and the collar tabs denoting the soldier's unit. Also, a distinctive cuff with Insignia representing a various award and the commendations. Completing with the uniform of a tall leather Jackboots and the iconic spiked pickelhaube helmet.

The uniform's attention to detail's, of a precise fit, and imposing appearance symbolising discipline and the formidable images of the German army during the First World War, introducing with both respect and fear in their adversaries.

The German soldiers are armed with the Gewehr 98 rifle, (Also known as the G-98.) Which was their standard-issue bolt-action rifle used by the German armies during the First World War.

It has a long barrel, wooden stock, and a five-round internal magazine. The rifle features of a powerful 7.92-millimetre calibre round and is renowned for its accuracy and reliability. Its rugged construction with an effective range has made it formidable weapon on the battlefield, allowing German soldiers to engage targets at long distance.

Now, let us focus on the uniform of Hauptmann (Captain), which serves as a symbol of authority and leadership within the German army. The officer's tunic is made of high-quality field grey wool, decorated with gold braids on the collar features with an embroidered rank insignia.

The tunic is complemented with matching trousers, often tucked into polished black leather boots. A visored peak cap, decorated with a cockade and officer's badge, completes the outfit. The meticulously tailored uniform embodies the prestige and responsibility that comes with the rank of Hauptmann and representing a commanding presence during the First World War battlefield.

As Robin and Martin's friends approach the edge of the Wee Loch, he catches sight of the German soldiers standing proudly in their distinctive uniforms. The soldiers issued with the iconic Holzer Stahl helm (a wooden Helmet) with a pointed top, reflects the moonlight and the highlight the battle scars engraved on the Holzer Stahl helm.

Among the German soldiers, Hauptmann Clink stands tall, his uniform decorated with various medals and insignias. He holds a G-98 rifle, a powerful weapon known for its accuracy, featuring a wooden stock contrast against moonlit surroundings. The polished wood has a subtle sheen, adding to the rifle's distinct appearance.

Hauptmann Clink, gripping the wooden stock of his G-98 rifle, turns to his comrades with a determine expression and shouts, "Ziel gesichtet! Feuer eröffen!" (Target spotted! Open fire!)

As the German soldiers prepares to carry out Hauptmann Clink's orders, Robin, and his friend swoops down and lands gracefully behind them. They remain hidden among the field of vibrant red poppies. The delicate wooden petals creaks with the wind, their slender stems swaying gently, providing a colourful and vivid backdrop to the tense scene. They exchange with an anxious glance, fully aware of the imminent danger and the urgency of their mission.

Martin, his voice filled with anxiety, whispers in Robin's ear, "They must not shoot! We must stop them!"

Robin flutters his wings and nods his little head in an agreement, surprising everybody, and begins chirping in flawless German, "Wir kommen in Frieden" (We come in peace). With an anxious expression, he shouts, "Bitte hört auf zu scießen!" (Please stop shooting.)

Lancer Schneider quickly turns his head and looks behind him, he notices the small birds among the wooden poppies. He stands in an astonishment. "Können die Vögel Deutsch sprechen?" (Can the birds speak German?)

Sergeant Schultz, squinting his eyes, rubbing his temples, is utterly bewildered. "Die Vögel sprechen, und sie sprechen Deutsch. Ich kann es kaum glauben!" (The birds are speaking, and they are speaking German. I can hardly believe it!)

Robin, understanding the Sergeant Schultz's astonishment, chirps once more. "Ja, Ja voll, wir können Deutsch sprechen und wir wollen Frieden." (Yes, we can speak German and we want peace.)

Hauptmann Clink opens his eyes in an astonishment, lowers his G-98 rifle and his troops did the same and he turns towards Robin cautiously. "Das ist unglaublich und was ist euer Zeil?" (This is incredible and what is your objective?)

Martin, doing his best to speak German, explains, "Wir Wollen Frieden. Kein Krieg Mehr. Die Zeiden des Kampfes Sind Vorobey. "(We are at peace. No more war. The fighting is now over.)

The German soldiers exchange with bewildered glances but find themselves captivate by the sincerity in Martin's eyes and a plea for peace.

Lancer Schneider moved by the birds' unexpected ability to communicate speaks softly, "Vielleicht sollten wir aufhören. Wenn diese Vögel für Frieden eintreten, Warrum sollten wir Dann kämpfen?"

(Perhaps. Perhaps we should stop. If these birds stand for Peace, why should we fight?)

Sergeant Schultz, with his scepticism melting away, nods in agreement. "Ich Denke, sie haben als Recht. Vielleicht ist es an der Zeit, einen anderen Weg zu finden." (I think, they are all right. Perhaps it's time to find a different path.)

Hold on with that thought, as a fragile sense of peace and understanding of non-violence begins to form. The language barriers fade as the German soldiers and the Birds converse in their shared tongue. Robin, with a flicker of hope in his heart, chirps softly with his message of peace resonating through the air. The German soldiers, once poised for battle, now contemplate the possibility of a different future. Well after sunset and the moonlight casts a warm glow over the scene, as a fragile, yet a powerful bond of peace and compassion are forged between the birds and the German soldiers.

The red poppies behind the German soldiers, stands for the symbols of remembrance and hope, serving as a reminder of lives lost and the importance of seeking peaceful resolutions. In Rozelle Park, amidst the remnants of a war-torn past, a flicker of hope ignites a spark with the potential to reshape their lives and the world around them.

As the Birds and the German soldiers stand in that poignant moment, they exchange introductions and stories. Hauptmann Clink, clicking his wooden boots, spoke first in broken English. "I'm Hauptmann Clink."

Robin, trying his best to communicate fluently in German, responds, "Ich bin Robin und Ich kann mit für Vögeln sprechen." (I am Robin, and I can speak for the Birds.)

Martin, also attempting to communicate in broken German, adds, "Ich bin Martin. Wir sind hier, um euch zu helfen." (I am Martin. We are here to help you.)

Sergeant Schultz, still struggling to comprehend the situation, mutters in his English, "I am Sergeant Schultz, I must be crazy! I have been talking to the Birds!"

Skittles, Tweety and Charlie Chirps in unison, introducing themselves with limited vocabulary and fragmented sentences, trying their best to communicate their intentions. Skittles: "Ich bin Skittles." Tweety: "Ich bin Tweety." Charlie: "Ich bin Charlie. "

Pepper as observant as ever, cuts in, with his broken German. "Wir kommen, um euch aus eurer Starre zu Befreunden. Ihr seid keine verbündeten." (We come to free you from your stare. You are not our allies.)

Hauptmann Clink, his curiosity piquing, asks in broken English. "How do the Birds speak German?"

Robin replies in fluent German, "Es ist seltsam, aber sie haben diese Fähigkeit geschenkt bekommen." (It is strange, but they have been gifted with this ability.)

The German soldiers, their expressions of mixed scepticism and fascination, struggled to process the unfolding events. The Birds, with their limited language skills and determination, became the messengers of hope. Bridging the language gap between the living and the statues.

Realising the significance of their encounter, Martin emphasises in his German, "Wir sind hier, um euch zu helfen. Gemeinsam können wir die Freiheit finden." (We are here to help you. Together we can find freedom.)

Robin, with a nod of understanding, takes flight and he soars through the night sky to find Major Tom. The news of the extraordinary turn of events weighs heavily on Robin's heart, urging them to share it. Rozelle Park is now pulsating with newfound energy and purpose, holds the promise of transformation and reconsideration. It transcends language barriers, uniting statues, and the carvings amidst the chaos.

As the sun begins to set on the first part of the book. Acorn, residing at the old oak tree, shares his thoughts with a gentle rustle of leaves. "Within these pages, you have witnessed the seeds of communication being sown, sprouting to life amidst the serene embrace of Rozelle Park. Through the extraordinary abilities of the Birds and the soldiers' newfound understanding, a bridge has been built, and Rozelle Park is now alive with untold stories waiting to unfold."

Acorn continues, his voice carrying a sense of anticipation, "But this is merely the beginning, dear readers. As you turn the pages of a future chapters, you will witness Rozelle Park brimming with adventures, friendships, and unexpected Connections. The statues and the carvings, once frozen in time, shall become characters of their own rights, embarking on a journey that intertwines with the living creatures of Rozelle Park."

With a hint of excitement, he concludes, "So, stay tuned. For Rozelle Park harbours countless secrets, and there are yet more tales to be revealed. As communication deepens and bonds strengthen, prepare yourselves for the wonders that lies ahead in in this enchanting world we call Roselle Park."

And with those words, the curtain falls on the first part of the book, leaving readers eagerly awaiting the unfolding events woven the magical tapestry of chapters yet to come.

Printed in Great Britain
by Amazon

27163542R00018